D1332426

Books by the same author

The Boy Who Walked on Water
Mary Poggs and the Sunshine
Singing to the Sun
The Thistle Princess and Other Stories
Under the Moon
Zenobia and Mouse

For younger readers

Lazy Jack
Princess Primrose
A Song for Little Toad
The Thistle Princess

TILLIE McGILLIE'S FANTASTICAL CHAIR

Climb aboard Tillie McGillie's fantastical chair and join her on her strange and uplifting adventures!

As a child Vivian French had a reputation for talking a lot. She made the most of this skill by becoming first an actor and then a storyteller, before discovering you could write stories down. She has now written more than one hundred and twenty books, including another Sprinter title, *Mary Poggs and the Sunshine* and several collections of stories such as *The Boy Who Walked on Water*; *The Thistle Princess and Other Stories*; *Under the Moon*; and *Singing to the Sun*. Vivian divides her time between Bristol and Edinburgh.

VIVIAN FRENCH
TILLIE McGILLIE'S
FANTASTICAL
CHAIR

Illustrations by
Sue Heap

WALKER BOOKS
AND SUBSIDIARIES
LONDON • BOSTON • SYDNEY

To Cathy and Susanna
with love
V.F.

First published 1992 by
Walker Books Ltd, 87 Vauxhall Walk
London SE11 5HJ

This edition published 2002

2 4 6 8 10 9 7 5 3 1

Text © 1992 Vivian French
Illustrations © 1992 Sue Heap

The right of Vivian French to be identified as author of this work
has been asserted by her in accordance with the
Copyright, Designs and Patents Act 1988

This book has been typeset in Garamond

Printed and bound in Great Britain by
The Guernsey Press Co. Ltd

British Library Cataloguing in Publication Data:
a catalogue record for this book is
available from the British Library

ISBN 0-7445-9052-3

Contents

Tillie McGillie lived at the very top
of a tall thin building with eighty-
two steps on the outside.

Tillie McGillie had
10 woolly hats

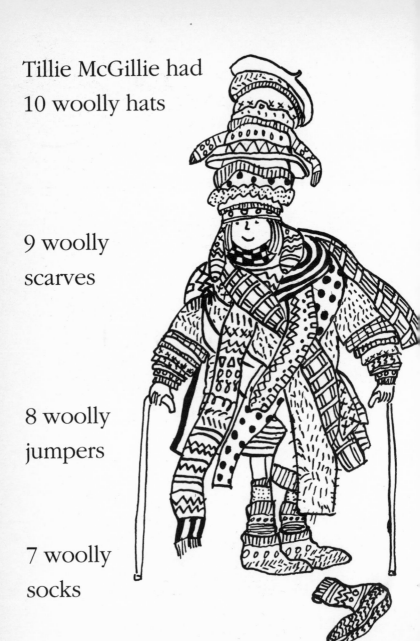

9 woolly
scarves

8 woolly
jumpers

7 woolly
socks

6 woolly cardigans

5 woolly blankets

4 knitting aunts

3 puffing uncles

2 wobbly legs   AND...

one gran who was nearly a fairy
and who came to tea as a surprise.

"Hello, Gran," said Tillie.

"H'mph," said Gran. "What's all
this woolliness?"

"It's my legs," Tillie explained. "The aunts like me to keep warm."

"Pots of tea need keeping warm," said Gran. "Children need fresh air."

Tillie sighed. "Carrying me up and down eighty-two steps makes the uncles puff so."

"H'mph," said Gran. "We'll see about *that*."

The aunts came hurrying in from the kitchen.

"Would you like some tea, Tillie's gran?" said Aunt Agnes.

"Shall we have some toast?" said Aunt Bridie.

"If we had known you were coming we would have made a special cake," said Aunt Clara.

"Are you warm enough, Tillie dear?" said Aunt Doris.

"H'mph," said Gran, very loudly, and she pulled a spotty hankie out of her pocket and waved it.

"OH! OH! OH! OH!" cried all the
aunts as they found themselves
circling round and round. Gran
waved the hankie again.

"OOOOOOOOOOOOOOOH!"
said all the aunts together as they
spun out of the front door and away
down the eighty-two steps.

The three uncles puffed in.

"What's all the noise about?" they asked.

Gran waved her hankie.

"Puff! Puff!" the uncles all shouted together. "Oh – Puff! Puff! Puff! PUFF!" And they joined hands in a line and went puffing down the stairs after the aunts.

"That's got rid of THEM," said Gran. "Now, child – what shall we do with you?"

"Is that a magic hankie? Are you going to wave it at me? Tillie asked anxiously.

"Not so easy," said Gran. She stared hard at Tillie's chair. "Is that comfortable?"

"Yes," Tillie said, wondering what was going to happen next.

Gran tapped the little red wheelchair on its back.

"H'mph – we can but try." She shut her eyes very tightly.

"*You can hop, you can skip, you can fly through the air –*
Tillie McGillie's fantastical chair!"

Tillie's chair gave a hop and
a skip.

"Hurrah!" Gran gave a little skip
herself. "Hold on tightly, Tillie!"

Tillie held on. The little red chair
gave a grunt, and a cough, and
sprang into the air.

"Up … up … up …" it said, in a
rusty dusty voice. "Up … up!"

Gran opened the
window wide.
"Fresh air," she
said firmly as the
chair and Tillie
flew past her.
"Don't forget now!"

Tillie saw Gran waving as the chair soared up into the sky above the building. She wanted to wave back, but she didn't dare let go.

"It's all right, you know," said
the dusty little voice of the chair.
"I won't drop you. You can wave
if you want to."

"Thank you," Tillie said
breathlessly, and waved.

"Wheeeee!" said the chair, and
flew up and over the roof of Tillie's
tall thin block of flats.

Tillie stared. Down below she could see the aunts running round and round after their wool, and the uncles were puffing up and down the eighty-two steps. Sometimes they met each other and then they would stop and bow, and say, "After you!" and, "No, no, dear Henry – after *you!*" but mostly they were too puffed to say anything at all.

Chapter
two

"Where to now?" asked the chair.
"North, south, east or west?"
"Up," said Tillie. "Up, up, up!"

"If you say so," said the chair, and
ZOOOOOM! up they went.

Two birds flying past were so
surprised that they bumped into
each other, and Tillie could hear
them squawking angrily behind her.

The chair began to slow down.
"Do you want to go MUCH higher?"
it asked in a breathless voice.

Tillie was about
to answer when there
was a loud and terrifying roar,
and something huge and silvery
rushed across the sky just above
her head. The little red chair spun
round and round in circles and
Tillie screamed as she held on as
tightly as she could.

"Dear me," said the chair,
steadying itself, "that was a near
thing. I feel quite shaken up!"

"Me too," said Tillie. "I don't think I like planes as close as that. Can we go down again?"

"We certainly can." The little red chair began to drop gently down, down, down until they were hovering just above the treetops.

"I can see a pond," Tillie said. "Can we go and look?"

The chair bobbed up and down, and swung Tillie through the air until they were over the pond. A group of children were busy with fishing nets and jamjars, and just as Tillie and the chair arrived a tall girl held up a jar full of small shining fish.

"Whatever are they catching?" Tillie asked. "Tiddlers," said the chair in a know-it-all voice.

"OH!" shouted Tillie. "OH – look at that little boy! He's just about to fall in – LOOK OUT! DO LOOK OUT!"

Tillie shouted in such a loud voice that all the children jumped and looked wildly around. There was the most enormous splash as not only the little boy but most of the other children fell into the

water, and they all began talking
and spluttering and waving their
arms about.

"Oh dear," Tillie said.

The chair made a quick turn
and shot off down the road. Tillie,
twisting round to see what was
happening, saw the children
scramble out of the pond and start
to chase after her, dripping trails of
weed and water behind them.

"STOP!" they shouted. "STOP!"
"Let's hide," said Tillie. "Quick!"

The chair swept up and over a
row of shops. A woman with two
girls came out of the greengrocer's
just as Tillie whizzed past, and she
let out a loud shriek and dropped
all her shopping. The two girls fell
over the heaps of potatoes and
cauliflowers and apples and sat
down on the pavement with a
flump.

"Oh dear, oh DEAR," said Tillie.
"WAIT FOR US!" shouted the
girls. The chair slid in between two
houses, and began to fly upwards.

"Where shall we go now?" Tillie asked. "None of the people down there like us very much – they keep wanting to chase us."

The little chair didn't answer, and Tillie suddenly noticed that instead of flying smoothly they were bumping from side to side and up and down.

"What's the matter?" Tillie patted the chair's arms.

"I think…" the chair wheezed, "that your gran's magic … is wearing … off…"

"Should we stop?" Tillie was anxious.

The chair took a deep breath.

"Let's … try … to get home," it said.

"Perhaps I could WISH us home," Tillie suggested.

"No harm in … trying," said the chair.

Tillie shut her eyes very tightly, and wished as hard as she could.

"I wish – I wish – I wish that Gran
  Would send us home as fast as
she can!"

Tillie opened her eyes. Nothing happened, but she saw that the chair was flying lower and lower, and giving strange hiccoughs and jerks as it went.

Tillie sat up straight. "Oh, look! We're nearly there!"

"Ohhhhh." The chair gave a small sigh, and landed gently on the ground in front of the tall thin building.

"What's the matter? Can't you fly any more?" Tillie patted and stroked the chair. "Dear chair – we had such fun – OH!"

Tillie stared. At the far end of the road she could see a group of children – a group of children all waving and running towards her.

Behind them was a woman waving
a shopping bag.

"It's those children who fell in
the pond … and the girls who sat
on the potatoes … and their mum!
Oh, little chair – what shall we do?"

The little red chair said nothing,
but Tillie felt it give the very faintest
jump.

"I KNOW!" Tillie leant forward,

and wriggled and slid out of the
chair until she was sitting on the
ground.

"There! Now you won't be so
heavy – can you fly? Fly up and
get Gran – tell her she's got to
come and help!"

The chair gave a little skip, and then a hop. Tillie held her breath, and shut her eyes, and wished as hard as she could.

"*You can hop, you can skip, you can fly through the air –*
Tillie McGillie's fantastical chair!"

There was a whoosh and a swoosh, and Tillie opened her eyes just in time to see the chair speeding up, up, up into the air.

At the same moment the children
arrived and all began shouting at
once. Then the aunts came hurrying
round the corner and started asking
Tillie WHAT ON EARTH SHE WAS
DOING, and the uncles puffed up
as well. They were much too puffed
to ask any questions, so they
pointed at Tillie and up at the sky

over and over again until Tillie felt
so battered and muddled by all the
noise and arm waving that she hid
her head in her hands and wished
as hard as she could that they
would all go away.

Chapter three

WHEEEEEEEEEEEEEEEEEEEEEE!

There was a sudden and total silence. Tillie peeped between her fingers. Gran was floating down, down, down from the top of the tall thin block of flats. She was sitting in Tillie's fantastical chair, and she was holding her spotty hankie.

"H'mph," she said. "Whatever's going on here?"

"Oh, Gran!" Tillie burst into tears. "I didn't mean to upset all these people! And the aunts and the uncles are all cross as cross can be with me!"

"The best way to help folks forget one thing is to give them another to remember," Gran said, and she waved her spotty hankie.

There was the

strangest noise that Tillie had ever heard. It sounded like a mountain pulling up its roots, or a gigantic monster heaving itself awake. The tall thin block of flats swayed, and shook, and trembled – and then rose slowly into the air.

Up it went, higher and higher – and
then it began turning and turning –
until it was upside down. Slowly,
slowly, it began coming down
again, and Tillie and all the others
gave a huge sigh as it settled back
down on the ground. It looked as if
it had always been there, firmly
rooted … but now it was upside
down.

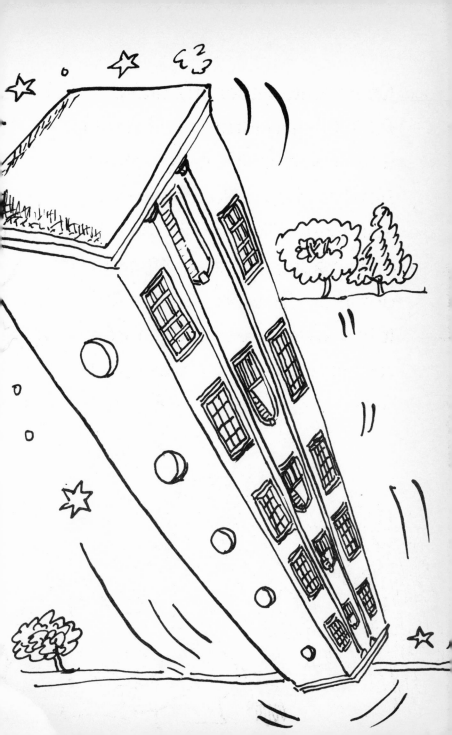

"There!" said Gran, looking very pleased with herself. "Now the uncles won't have to carry you up and down eighty-two steps.

You can wheel yourself in and out just as you please, Tillie McGillie, so there'll be a lot less woolliness and a lot more fresh air. Oh, and don't go worrying yourself about upside-down furniture." Gran waved her hankie a couple more times. "There! It's all as right as ninepence! Go and see!"

Gran helped Tillie back into the little red chair, and Tillie trundled herself into her flat through what had been a front door at the very top of the building … but was now a front door at the bottom. The uncles and aunts crowded after her, still too surprised to say anything.

"It's LOVELY!" said Tillie, looking round.

Gran nodded. "So it is," she said.

The children who had fallen in the pond came rushing in.

"Yippee!" they said. "It's magic! We live right at the top of the flats now, just where we always wanted to, so we can look at the stars at night!" And they all rushed out again to look up at their new, high-up windows.

The woman with the shopping bag and the two girls knocked at the door.

"Good afternoon," she said. "So nice to have new neighbours… We live in the middle flat, you know. Charmed to meet you … perhaps Tillie would like to play with Susie and Sally sometimes?"

Tillie looked at the girls. She saw that they still had dirty knees from falling over, but they smiled at her.

"Do come," they said together, 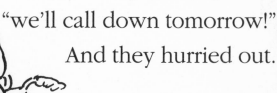 "we'll call down tomorrow!"

And they hurried out.

Tillie rubbed her nose. "Why aren't they cross any more, Gran?" she asked.

"Like I said," said Gran. "Give folks something new to think of, and they'll forget everything else as like as not." She coughed, and

nodded at the aunts and uncles who were skittering about, admiring the new ceilings and floors. "Look at them – they've quite forgotten I've come to tea," she said.

"Well," Tillie said, "they have
been rather busy since you came.
I'll make the tea for you."

She went towards the kitchen,
and then turned back. "Gran," she
said, "thank you very much."

"H'mph," said Gran, pulling her spotty hankie out of her pocket.

"Whoops!" said Tillie, and rolled herself quickly into the kitchen … but Gran was only using her hankie to wipe her spectacles.

"H'mph," Gran said to herself quietly. "I'm wiping my spectacles THIS time … but the NEXT time I use my spotty hankie … who knows?" And she winked at the little red chair as Tillie came back with the tea things.

More _SPRINTERS_ for you to enjoy!

- *Captain Abdul's Pirate School* Colin McNaughton 0-7445-5242-7

- *The Ghost in Annie's Room* Philippa Pearce 0-7445-5993-6

- *Molly and the Beanstalk* Pippa Goodhart 0-7445-5981-2

- *Taking the Cat's Way Home* Jan Mark 0-7445-8268-7

- *The Finger-eater* Dick King-Smith 0-7445-8269-5

- *Care of Henry* Anne Fine 0-7445-8270-9

- *Cup Final Kid* Martin Waddell 0-7445-8297-0

- *Lady Long-legs* Jan Mark 0-7445-8296-2

- *Patrick's Perfect Pet* Annalena McAfee 0-7445-8911-8

- *Me and My Big Mouse* Simon Cheshire 0-7445-5982-0

- *No Tights for George!* June Crebbin 0-7445-5999-5

- *Art, You're Magic!* Sam McBratney 0-7445-8985-1

- *Ernie and the Fishface Gang* Martin Waddell 0-7445-7868-X

- *Elena the Frog* Dyan Sheldon 0-7445-8960-6

- *Hector the Rat* Tony Wilkinson 0-7445-9033-7

- *Little Stupendo Rides Again* Jon Blake 0-7445-9051-5

- *The Polecat Café* Sam Llewellyn 0-7445-9028-0

- *Tillie McGillie's Fantastical Chair*
  Vivian French 0-7445-9052-3

All at £3.99